QUEEN OF SOULS
LA CALACA

by

Kristen Collins

Layout and design by No Sweat Graphics & Formatting
Editor: Susette at My Write Hand VA

Printed in the United States of America
ISBN:

Table of Contents

Prologue: Origin of La Calaca i
Halloween 1
All Saints Day 21
All Souls Day 35
Epilogue: Destiny 67
About the Author 78

Prologue: Origin of La Calaca

"From my rotting body, flowers shall grow and I am in them and that is eternity."
- Edvard Munch

Hello there, my name is Mictecacihuatl. It's kind of a mouth full so you can call me Mic for short. Everyone does, but I have been called many names in my time: La Catrina, La Calaca or even just Death. In some cultures, I have been worshipped as a goddess but mostly I'm just a Fairer, a caretaker for souls. There are other Death Angels but I am the sole ruler of death for both my domain and people, anyone of Aztec origin. When they die, they go to Mictlan to spend eternity.

The way humans dress up and put makeup on these days is, in a way, a symbol of who I am. My entire body was covered in ink, black to shade my skin and white to make me look like a skeleton from head to toe. Although in the beginning, our clothes were of that time, as civilization advanced on earth, so did we in Mictlan. The entire land was built era on top of each era that had passed since the beginning of time. I have been pleased with the way the souls of my people have been able to adapt to the changes that come every few decades now.

During Halloween, the veil between the living and the dead becomes thin, and by midnight the gates of Mictlan open. First, the souls of the children are allowed to return to their families. After they return back to Mictlan by midnight of *El Dia de los Inocentes*, the adults take their turn back with their families for *All Souls Day*.

These three days are the most stressful, yet heartwarming, moments I get to experience in my existence. From the moment the gates of Mictlan open up at midnight on Halloween, I observe in my realm the happy reunions and time humans spend with the souls of their loved ones that have left. The souls are forever tethered to me. I can feel if they ever feel a hesitation about not coming back.

To leave them on earth would prove disastrous for them. Soul Eaters lurk in the human realm searching for a lost soul to devour. To protect them, each soul of Mictlan is accompanied by their spirit animal as they wander back to their loved ones, enabling them to spend their time back home without any worries or issues.

Loved ones that still live make *ofrendas* and light paths to guide the spirits back to their homes. The four elements- fire, earth, wind, and water are required of every offering. They spend all day Halloween preparing various fruits and dishes, setting up their ofrendas.

Salt not only shows purification but encircles the altar and pathway. Multiple tiers hold each of the different offerings to the souls of their loved ones. Of the element earth, crops are the representation. The aroma of the fresh harvest feeds the souls; birds feast on the scratch and seeds left on the altar. Tissue paper is often the object representing the wind. It's paper thin and lightweight, easily swaying in the breeze. The Papel Picado, or tissue paper as some humans call it, is cut into the shape of butterflies and other symbolic icons such as sugar skulls and flowers.

Pitchers of water sit beside empty glasses so souls can quench their thirst after the long journey from Mictlan. Of course, lit candles would come to represent fire, although some families build small fires as well in either pits in the ground or fire places. Copal, also known as incense, burns to guide the souls, purifying them after their journey home. Eccentric rugs are freshly made every year and placed on the ground at the foot of the ofrenda for the souls to sit and rest on when they arrive.

The most symbolic feature that is well known are the marigolds that are weaved and placed on the pathway to the altar for the soul's final journey into the homes. It is said that whenever a soul may become lost, that the scent of the marigolds will guide, or rather lure, them back to the path or an altar that their loved ones have prepared for them. When the souls return back to Mictlan, butterflies flock throughout the villages assuring the families that their loved ones made it back to the Underworld safely.

Every day in Mictlan is Dia de los Muertos and the bridge between the living and the dead is always covered in marigolds. We have candle makers that keep our city lit every night and we feast as one giant family daily. The souls are happy and at peace here in Mictlan. Their spirit animals always keep watch to protect the realm.

What about me, you ask? What does the Queen of Souls receive after it's all said and done? I ask for nothing but my souls usually bring me something back from earth as a thank you. Protecting and guiding their souls is my purpose and reason for my existence. The Creator made me just for them, like He made Sandmen for protecting dreams and Angels to watch over and protect the humans.

To better understand how I came to be or what I am, then I must take you back first, back to where it all began.

******

"Rise, Mictecacihuatl. Rise, I say! Rise as Queen of Souls!" the Creator commanded.

As an Angel of Death, I was chosen for a special assignment by the Creator Himself but I had to undergo a transformation only He could perform.

Helping me to my feet, He led me to still water, "Look at your new form."

Peeking into the beautifully clear water, I observed my new form and I saw that I no longer looked like I once was. My body was covered in black and white so that I looked more skeletal but I was still beautiful. At least, those were my thoughts but I kept them to myself.

I had been assigned to become the protector to the Aztecs in the human realm, they had acquired their own land in the afterlife after the Europeans brought nothing but pestilence and war to their front door. I didn't ask questions, only accepted the gracious offer extended to me. My new look was shocking at first but it wasn't hard for me to accept it.

Looking over my body and seeing myself for the first time, I could feel the new power I was bestowed with, pumping throughout my veins. The power was enticing and exhilarating even.

"What's wrong? Are you unhappy with your new form, Mictecacihuatl?" He asked when I realized I had not spoken yet.

"No, Creator. I love it, I just didn't expect to look so..."

"Different?" He chuckled, illuminating his presence more.

"Yes but I'll adjust. What do you want me to do first?" I asked.

""You don't just look different but every molecule of your being has been reconstructed to suit your new role in Mictlan. Rule your realm, protect the Aztec people and the souls that come after. They will become your people and like a shepherd, you will be charged to guide them and keep the wolves from devouring them. The human realm has some creatures that have been attacking the souls when they return for twenty-four hours once a year."

"What if I need you? Or help? What do I do then?" I inquired.

"Each soul will have their own protector that should aid in protecting them but if something happens, I have equipped you to be able to handle any situation that could occur," He answered.

"Am I banned from heaven? Forever?" I was saddened by the thought of never seeing the Creator again.

"No, child. And I am always with you, no matter what may happen. Now go. Your souls, your charges await you."

I bowed in respect, leaving his realm for the last time.

Halloween

Silence is an empty space, space is the home of the awakened mind.
- Gautama Buddha

~ La Llorona ~

For centuries, I have wandered this earth aimlessly, looking for the souls of my children whom I murdered in a fit of regrettable blind rage. With every face I look into, all I see are my children but after the fantasy leaves, I realize they are not my children and then the rage comes back. I completely black out only to come to and see the children dead because of my hands.

I am only able to wander the earth from Purgatory three days a year- Halloween and the two days of Dia de los Muertos: All Saints Day and All Souls Day. The Purgatory prison that has held me all the other days of the year is torturous.

This year is different. This year, I will find my children and be reunited with them for all eternity. If I want my suffering to end then I have to make things right with them but nothing will ever be right if I can't find them. The only way to find them is to kidnap all the souls of the children that leave Mictlan to be reunited for twenty-four hours with their descendents, their living relatives that make ofrendas for their ancestors.

To gather all the souls of the children from Mictlan is no easy task though. They all have spirit animals that protect them from any entity that dares to steer their path away from their destinations.

I've been left with no choice but to enlist the help of the despicable Soul Eaters in order to get what I want. I've made a deal with them. What's a few souls of some children in order to get my children back? To me, it was worth the trade, the risk to end my eternity of suffering.

The Louisiana bayou was an easy place for anything living or dead to disappear within. It can be very unforgiving. Deep within, I relate to this marshy place on various levels. The whole day of Halloween had been painful waiting for night to descend as I searched out the Soul Eaters and struck a deal, with an offering of my own to them, of course. But in this case, the enemy of my enemy is my friend.

The Soul Eaters drifted aimlessly waiting to go on the prowl. Midnight was fast approaching and they were hungry for the souls that would soon leave Mictlan. I had to already send them off for quick snacks after the sun set on All Hallows Eve, the greedy nasty creatures. Cursed with endless hunger that made their ability to control their urges near impossible.

"Nicholi!" I screeched as the leader of the Soul Eaters came to my side.

"Yesssss...." His answer drew out.

"Gather your fellow creatures, tell them to get into position. The hunt is about to begin. They are not to touch any child's soul but anything else is fair game," I ordered with a wave of my hand.

The responding crackles and hisses answered in delight at my order. Within seconds, they began to dispatch throughout the bayou.

"Go!" I screamed, "Find me my babies and bring them back to me!" I began to wail, it was the only relief I have ever known since my death. The banshee scream echoed throughout the night.

I waited until they left to allow a moment for myself, the images of my dead children's faces haunt me every second of my existence.

The day started out so promising, the weather was beautiful and not a cloud in sight in the sky. I noticed my husband forgot his tools at home.

Things have been so tense at home lately that I packed a few extra treats to bridge my apologies. All I wanted was to get us back to where we once were. Losing our youngest child a year ago was the wedge that divided us but I love him and don't want to live like this anymore. Today, I would put my sorrow behind me and work hard for us both to overcome the grief that crushes us every day.

Down the dirt path, I walked to his shop in the village. Because it can be so noisy, he planted it off at the edge of town.

I snuck in through the back door and adjusted my dress so that it was perfectly presentable for him when I surprise him.

Laughter caught my attention. At first, I thought it was a customer laughing at one of his ridiculous jokes but then it never stopped, only faded to hushed whispers.

Quietly, I tip-toed across the room and toward his office door. It was barely cracked but it was open enough for me to see the arms of another woman wrapped around my husband. She wrapped her soft hands around his neck and raised her lips to his ears, whispering sweet words. He closed his eyes, inhaling the scent of her perfume as my heart shattered. With each sound, each touch between them, I lost another piece of my heart. The very fabric of my being threatening to disintegrate until there was nothing left.

That smile...That was my smile, the one he reserved for me and me alone. I didn't run but my heart pumped faster and beat against my chest as if it were about to burst. I let the tears fall but my feet felt like they were glued to the floor. The pressure from me trying to move on the floor allowed for the boards to creak under my feet.

The moment of dread finally hit, my husband's eyes and I locked with each other. His mouth opened to speak but nothing came out, My feet finally unlocked and I bolted out of the shop and back toward the house.

Everything became a blur after that. The wails that escaped my lips echoed throughout the village. Everything was just a quick flash of a face or feeling but no sound came to my ears, only the sound of unbearable silence.

I blacked out, my brain just went blank. I don't know for how long either but the sound of people screaming my name brought me to.

Their voices sounded so far away but why was I in the river? Looking around, my husband and brother were pulling others out of the water. Were those bodies?

"What's going on?" I asked, my voice muddled, tapping on my mother-in-law's shoulder.

My mother-in-law was crying and wailing, she turned to look at me. "Why, Mija? Why did you hurt the children?"

"Wh-what? My...children?" My senses snapped into place finally as I pushed past her and ran over to my children's lifeless bodies on the ground.

My husband's pain was crushing as he accused, "Why didn't you take me?! They were innocent!"

I backed away from them, unable to process what I had done. Looking around, the mob was forming, calling for my head.

They were right, I deserved to die for what I did. I didn't mean to hurt them, I just lost control... The waterfall was within running distance. My feet led the way before my brain connected the dots.

If I could just make it a little further, the ending to my pain was waiting for me. I can end the suffering by jumping off the waterfall. The bottom of the water was my savior, I just can't take it anymore.

I leapt off the rock that was the step of my life, my arms extended out as if I was soaring through the air, but it was only a split second before there was a painful jolt throughout my body and then there was nothing.

~ Papa Legba ~

"The cards are telling me that you will find wealth and prosperity through your new job, happiness, and a family too," I told the tourist, looking over her tarot cards.

"So Peter and I will have a family?!" She smiled, looking over at her disbelieving boyfriend as he huffed disapprovingly.

I flipped another card, "With Peter? No."

Her brows furrowed in confusion as she laughed nervously, "What do you mean, Papa Legba? There must be some mistake because we're getting married in a few months."

"No, cher. I am not mistaken, the cards don't lie. You see, Peter here has been sneaking around with your Maid of Honor. She is with child as we speak. She is trying to figure out how to tell him," I answered and the bride's eyes welled with tears and her shoulders slumped in defeat.

Peter shot up out of his chair, "You're a con artist! Honey, let's go. He's full of crap."

"Am I now? You see, my friends on the other side see things you don't think anyone else knows about because you think the things you do in the dark go unnoticed but that's not true. You may want to get that call. It's very important news from the Maid of Honor." I shrugged nonchalantly.

Peter's pocket started to vibrate as he took his phone from his pocket. The name Katherine read on the phone as the bride snatched the phone from him, walking away, screaming into it.

"Kat, is it true? Are you pregnant with Peter's child?!" she accused, wailing into the phone.

Apologies, tears, and confusion answered her in return as she launched the phone across the room at Peter.

"Baby...It's not true. They're all lying. I bet Katherine put him up to it. You know how jealous she is of our relationship...," he lied but the bride was having no part of it.

"Get out! The wedding is off!" she screamed at him. He reached for her but she screamed even louder, hollering at him, "Leave! Now! I can't even look at you!" she said in disgust.

"Whatever." He waved her off, snatching his phone from the ground, throwing the door open and disappearing out onto the streets of the French Quarter.

"I am so sorry you had to see that," she apologized.

"'Tis not your fault, cher. I will leave you with a parting secret. Mr. Right is the real best friend. He has always been there since you both were children. He's currently at Cafe Du Monde right now enjoying some coffee and beignets. If you hurry, you can catch him."

She sniffled, wiping her running nose on her sleeve. "Thank you, Papa Legba." The bride dropped the money onto the table and turned around, leaving out the front of my voodoo shop.

Chatter began to commence amongst the shrunken voodoo heads hanging around the shop. Their eyes began to glow and their voices were a jumble of chaos and fear.

"As a mediator, it would be great if I could hear what each of you had to say but you know I can't understand a word coming from any of you when you all start chattering at the same time." I rolled my eyes in annoyance. They do this every time, I swear.

Whispers sounded around me, different voices sprouting one or two words at a time. I sat at my table with my crystal ball in the center of it, mumbling incantations to bring the voices' words to life.

"Chaos...pain...suffering..." they all said in unison.

"Rebellion..." another head whispered.

The ball brought forth life within, showing me what was going to happen out on the streets around the world. One by one the spirit animals of the children of Mictlan were bound and the children were placed in a trance. The location looked familiar but I wasn't sure exactly where just yet.

"Soul Eaters...La Llorona..."

"The souls of the children of Mictlan are in danger..."

"Mic's realm is under attack? The souls of the children?" I asked in confusion.

"The Queen of Souls must be warned..."

"Yes, you must help stop the souls from being stolen...," they continued to whisper.

"When will this take place? The gates of Mictlan won't open until midnight on Halloween," I asked but the hissing reply was what I needed to know. *I must investigate this matter more.* I thought to myself. I need to warn Mic but there is no way until the gates open.

Grabbing my top hat and slinging my suit jacket over my shoulder, I took off into the streets of New Orleans. I needed to warn the others at least and the one place where all creatures would end up is Marie Laveau's bar, The Voodoo Lair.

The music was inviting and the sweet smell of incense welcomed me to my sister's bar. Marie was sitting at the end of the bar counting money when I strolled inside.

Making my way over to her and taking a seat on the bar stool, I waved the bartender down. No need to tell them what to bring me as I was a regular here nightly.

"I know that mood." Marie said, without even looking up from the piles of money she was counting. "You've either done something or you're about to do something stupid," she quipped.

I twirled the cold drink around between my fingers, "More like I know of something that is about to happen and there is nothing I can do to stop it, Marie."

Marie paused and looked up, "You wouldn't be coming to me unless your friends from the other side didn't think it was nothing."

"Mic and her charges are in trouble. Something is going to kidnap the souls of the children of Mictlan on All Saints Day." My mouth vomited the rest of my vision and warning I received in my shop earlier.

Marie listened intently to every word. "There has not been a Soul Eater attack in New Orleans since..." She started but stopped, unable to finish her sentence.

"It's okay, Marie. Since they killed Octavio and Hazel. I have to tell myself everyday it's okay to say their names and talk about them but when the pain becomes too much..." He held up his drink, "I have something to kill the pain in order to get some sleep again.

"One of these days you and Mic will be able to forgive yourselves and each other. She just needs more time," Marie coaxed and I slammed my fist down on the bar top.

"More time? It's been decades, Marie! And not once has she checked on me to see if I was surviving. She was not the only one who lost her children that night! They were my children too! I didn't just lose my children that night but my wife! My soulmate!"

Marie reached out and squeezed my hand in hers, "I know, Brother." Taking a deep breath, she asked, "What do you need from me?"

"I need you to use your gift of sight and find a way to warn her. We cannot reach her in Mictlan and the spirits from the other side will not get any more involved. But we have to get word to her before it's too late," I said desperately.

"Do not fret, Brother. I will find a way to get the message to Mic. We may not be able to stop what is about to happen but we can help her through it, undo what the Soul Eaters and La Llorona plan to carry out," she reassured me.

"Thank you, Sister. I must get back to my shop. I need to see what else I can get from my friends on the other side. We should also increase the patrol of our supernatural friend connections throughout the French Quarter. The last thing we need is for any more of our children to go missing," I urged and Marie agreed. I grabbed the bottle of liquor and headed back out the door to return to my shop.

Forgive me, Mic. I wish I could do more for you, my love.

~ Mic ~

Longing filled my soul knowing what tomorrow meant, especially on the anniversary of the deaths of my children. Sharp pains filled my body and I fell onto my knees on the floor of my home. My body felt as if I was being torn in two.

My lady that assisted me in everything daily, rushed to my side, "Your Majesty! Are you all right?"

I reached out and took Felicia's hands as she helped pull me to my feet and over to my sitting chair by the window. A gentle breeze blew through, easing the wave of nausea that was starting to overcome me.

"Thank you, Felicia. I'm all right, I think the impending day of tomorrow has gotten the best of me," I answered honestly to my confidante and friend.

"You do too much, Your Highness. Always going and never stopping to rest or take care of yourself," she tsked, chastising me because she was displeased with my workaholic self as always. "One of these days, you will finally listen to me and take some time for yourself again."

I laughed at her frustration, "My old friend, there is no such thing as rest anymore for me. There are so many souls I must manage and I'm afraid if I stop then I may come undone again.

Especially with what tomorrow is, you know I am always barely holding myself together on this day every year."

Felicia looked at me knowingly, kneeling before me, "Maybe you should once again visit the realm of the living like you used to do."

Scoffing at her I asked, "And do what exactly?"

"When was the last time you spoke with Papa Legba or Marie Laveau?" she inquired.

I slunk further into my chair, "I doubt they want anything to do with me."

She raised an eyebrow at my answer, "How so, my Lady?"

"Let's just say the last time I spoke with either of them, my words were not so kind. In fact, I'm pretty sure, if my memory serves me correctly, that my wrathful side took over and just ran rampant on all who I encountered," I answered vaguely but Felicia knew what that meant for all who I came into contact with when that part of me was in charge.

"I see but let me ask you this. Would a man that knew full in advance what you were capable of and that you share children with be really capable of dismissing you at the worst time of your life?" she paused, waiting for my answer.

"I honestly don't know what he's capable of anymore, Felicia. I don't want to discuss it anymore. The Voodoo King and I are done. We were done the night my children died under his roof after he swore they were safe from harm," I said bitterly.

Felicia nodded in understanding, "Well then, I will only say one more thing and not another word about it." She waited until I looked her in the eye before continuing, "If that was all it took for him to dismiss the love you two shared, then it wasn't true love after all. Real love means throughout all tribulations, no matter how harsh they may be; that you will be there in the end for one another no matter the cost, or wrath, the other may endure."

As she stood up and walked off, I looked out the window once more pondering over her words. Maybe she was right? I would never know because I had no intention of leaving Mictlan unless I absolutely had to. I rather enjoyed my view from my home looking out the window and watching the children continuing the living tradition of trick or treating.

I smiled at the children as they wandered the streets in homemade costumes going from house to house and even to the street vendors trick and treating as they all were given candy and they jumped up and down in excitement.

What I loved about it is that the spirit animals, although annoyed at first when we started this new human tradition in Mictlan, have grown accustomed to making their children happy by participating in the candy scavenger hunting event. They even allowed their children to put costumes on them, although they were beautiful and something out of a human magazine already. They each glowed in the dark and were full of vibrant colors and markings.

Seeing the joy and peace my people felt in the streets of Mictlan made my internal suffering worth it even more. Because of them, I can keep on moving forward in order for them to have peace. It's the sacrifice, as the Queen of Souls, I must make daily.

With a sharp intake of a painful breath, I let the sweet memory fill me...

I doubled over with my hands on my knees as another wave of contractions came. Gritting my teeth, I screamed out in pain as my belly tightened and I felt one of the twins slide down further in the birthing canal.

Milayna held one hand with her other holding my arm firmly, Felicia held the other as we made our way toward the gates of Mictlan.

"The babies are coming! We're not going to make it, Your Majesty!" Felicia said with a voice full of doubt.

Blowing air through my gritted teeth, "Yes, we will!" Another scream came from my lungs, my hair was soaked with sweat as I forcibly made my legs move forward one step at a time.

"The Voodoo King will be with me when the children arrive," I vowed.

"This is enough." Milayna whistled to the onlooking crowd of spectators that were anxiously awaiting the arrival of the first children to be born in Mictlan. She ordered "Come here and help the Queen through the gates, The Voodoo King awaits on the bridge."

Juan and Franco along with a few others came to my aid, gently lifting me in the air as they rushed me through the gates where an anxious Papa Legba was pacing back and forth.

When his eyes fell on me as the men laid me on top of the soft marigold bridge, they backed away. I had never been more grateful for the souls that remained behind these days instead of returning to the human realm.

He knelt beside me. More souls of women came rushing out the gate with pillows, blankets and water.

Papa Legba looked admirably at me, "Cher, you're doing great!" he encouraged me.

I half-laughed, huffing and gritting my teeth, as Felicia handed me a leather wrapped spool, "Here, My Lady, bite down on this for the pain."

"I thought I was going to miss all the excitement," he joked.

"If I..." I panted, pausing in between words with the leather still between my teeth, "Have to

suffer through this birth...then you're going to feel every ounce of pain with me.

Milayna propped my knees up, ordering Flora and Mya to hold them up. The motion made one of the twins slip further down and a flaming, burning sensation took over. "What...is...that?!" I panted.

"What are you feeling?" Milayna asked.

"It burns!" I screamed.

Was I being ripped in half? Were these children going to claw their way out of me?

Milayna chuckled at me, "That is the shoulders, the first baby's head is crowning. Now on the next contraction, I need you to push really hard."

I shook my head, "I...I can't, Milayna. The pain is too much," I cried as Papa Legba squeezed my hands.

"Nonsense. You can and you will," she commanded firmly.

She placed a hand on my belly, feeling for another contraction. When my belly tightened and the pain shot throughout my body, I wailed and cried out again.

"Push, Your Majesty. Push like your life depends on it."

"Push, cher! I'm right here beside you," Papa Legba urged.

I tried but the pain was just too much and I shook my head feeling defeated.

"Mic..." He paused before continuing with his next words, "I am going to ease your pain, my love."

He muttered some indecipherable words as I tightened my grip on his hands but the pain seemed to subside to bearable.

Spitting the leather spool from my mouth, I looked up at him noticing he was gritting his teeth and it wasn't from my grip on his hand, "What did you do, mi amor?"

He smiled down at me, "I took on some of your pain to help you through this.

"Push, Your Majesty. It's time and the baby needs to come now!" Milayna ordered again.

With all the strength I could muster, I pushed feeling one of the twins slip through and out. Screams from me echoed around us as Papa Legba grunted through the pain he took.

One twin cried immediately upon birth as Felicia snatched the child away, working clearing the airway. With a pat on the butt, the child's cries made my heart ease in relief, "It's a boy!"

I didn't have time to celebrate when the burning sensation came again and I screamed. Milayna quickly looked and frowned, working away but I was starting to feel weak.

Papa Legba noticed the look on Milayna's face as well. "Is there a problem?" he asked.

"The other child is coming too fast and she's losing a lot of blood. I'm not sure she even has enough strength to deliver the second child at this point," she answered honestly with a look of worry on her face.

I was feeling pretty woozy. Even sleepiness started taking over me, but with the last bit of strength I had within me, I pushed with everything I had left.

The pressure released finally as Milayna held up the other twin to Felicia but the child was crying the second she was born.

"It's a girl and she's feisty," Felicia laughed.

Felicia handed the boy over to Papa Legba and she laid the girl on my chest, supporting my arms.

"What should we name them, mi amor?" I asked weakly.

"Hazel Ann for our daughter?" he asked and I nodded.

"Octavio Legba for our son?" I asked and he chuckled agreeing. "Happy birthday, Octavio and Hazel. Welcome to the world."

Such a memorable moment in my life, all of my life was full of them but only certain ones replayed on a loop when my eyes closed every night. Unfortunately, not all those memories are as precious as this one that I visited today.

ALL SAINTS DAY

The warm summer breeze blew the smell of freshly bloomed flowers around the air. Octavio and Hazel were playing hide and seek. My little spider monkey, Hazel, was sitting on a tree branch looking down at her big brother, barely containing her laughter as he searched around blindly for her.

"Hazel! Where are you?" Octavio whined in frustration.

He caught her hiding up, just slightly out of reach, dangling from a tree branch upside down, giggling uncontrollably.

"Mama! She's doing it again! Hazel, that's not fair!" Octavio accused.

Hazel shrugged nonchalantly, "You need to think outside the box, Bubba."

"Awe, cher, our little family is quite the entertainment, are they not?" Papa Legba chuckled beside me.

"Agreed. She gets her clever skills from you, mi amor," I giggled.

"Would you like another beignet, my love?" The Voodoo King held one out for me to take a bite.

Graciously, I took a nibble of the sweet bread, lifting up some white wine to sip. Something started to seem off though, I took another glance at the wine noticing it wasn't white at all but red. A deep, crimson red at that, was it thicker?

"Legba, you know I don't drink red wine..." I muttered confused.

Legba didn't say a word as I looked up, he and the twins stood without moving, only staring back at me, wide-eyed.

Everything around me began to distort as I looked down again, bringing the wine closer to my eyes.

"This...this isn't wine," I objected but yelled to my son, "Octavio, get your sister! We need to leave right now!"

It was blood I noticed, feeling shocked and chunking it across the open meadow.

"What is wrong with you, Papa Legba? We need to get the children!"

I grabbed his wrist as an unknown fear inched up my spine threatening to consume me. When he wouldn't budge, I rushed over to Octavio and Hazel, who somehow managed to get onto the ground while I was distracted.

They remained almost lifeless where they stood side by side. Rushing toward them, I fell before them, grabbing at them.

"Did you hear me, children? We have to leave now!" Shaking their arms, they didn't respond, "Why are you not moving! Why are you not answering me?"

Eerily, they both looked at me in unison, barely opening their mouths as if to speak and blood began to pour from between their lips before disintegrating into dust.

My hand ran through the piles of what were my children on the ground as I screamed, "Octavio? Hazel? Babies! Where are you?!"

Grief and despair took over me from inside out, letting the pain rip me in two.

"My Lady?" A voice reached through before I felt hands on my shoulder shaking me awake, "My Lady! Your Majesty, you have to wake up!" Felicia pleaded, jolting me awake finally.

"Felicia?" I reached out and latched onto her, tears falling in a steady stream. "They were there, Felicia."

"Who, My Lady?" Felicia asked, confused.

"Octavio and Hazel!" I cried and Felicia's grip tightened around me in understanding as she shushed me.

The chiming of the clock of time signaled the end of Halloween was near.

Mentally, I sent out a simple note to them, *Happy Birthday, my darlings. Wherever you may be now...*

Time was not measured in this realm as humans measure time in their realm. I once tried to explain it to a human bartender that worked in a bar that us supernaturals frequented when stopping by the human realm. I soon learned it was only something that would make sense once their souls crossed over into the afterlife.

******

The large clock chimed midnight as the children hugged their family members that care for them in Mictlan until their parents or siblings arrive here when they die.

"Layla." I nodded at the young one. "I hope you enjoy your time with your Papa and Mama. I know they have been missing you a lot, dear.

"Thanks, Mic. I can already taste my Mama's tortillas." She pointed to her wide open mouth, "See! It's already watering!" she giggled.

The chuckles escaped me at her excited giddiness, "Yes indeed, I see! You better get going before Paca leaves you and takes all of your mama's tortillas for herself!" I teased as her mouth dropped and she gasped.

She turned abruptly looking for her spirit animal, "Paca! Wait! You come back here right now!" She ran after Paca, as her spirit animal jogged slowly so she could catch up to her.

More children took off running across the marigold bridge, some giggly while others focused on their journey home, and a few pulled the buddy system with our child souls from Mictlan. I glanced back at the adults as they watched in ease with the spirit animals tailing behind or flying above the children.

Once the children had been gone a while, it was my turn to celebrate All Saints Day in the only way I could. I reached down and grabbed the large basket I had placed by the gate earlier before the send off.

One by one, I pulled out photographs of my children, Octavio and Hazel. The twins were always so beautiful, both held bits and pieces of mine and their father's features. A tear fell down my cheek and then another as I set up the ofrenda in their memory. Unlike the rest of the world, my children would not return to me, their souls were gone forever.

I placed their favorite meals on the ofrenda and lit the candles around their photos. Once everything was in place I just knelt down and took out the last thing for the altar, voodoo dolls their father had made for them as babies. Paella came up to me, nudging me with her big horse nose.

"Hey, Paella." I turned and wrapped my arms around her thick neck as her wings engulfed me in an embrace.

I lifted my eyes and saw that the adults that were here, waiting back in respect of my mourning, but each one of them held something to honor my ofrenda I had made for my children.

They looked at one another nervously as I nodded to them, welcoming them into my space. As always, every year they mourned with me in my loss. They were the ones to help me heal and put myself back together after their deaths. They understand the pain and suffering I endured and the peace they knew I would never receive with the loss of my babies.

Milayna came to me as I sat on a patch of marigolds and placed food down beside me. I tried to push it away but she shook her head, "You must eat something tonight too, Your Majesty."

She placed a gentle hand on top of my shoulder as I reached up and squeezed it in comfort, "Milayna, you always take such good care of me every year. Thank you, my friend."

She smiled and patted me, before walking away, Paella plopped down beside me like the diva she was. A **Pegasus** was quite the large animal, and for my spirit animal, she was everything I was and more but on the outside versus me who kept it all bottled in…mostly.

"I'm assuming you're wanting some of Milayna's famous tortillas, eh?" I laughed when she huffed in response, making me shake my head at her.

Sitting there, holding onto their voodoo dolls I held them up to my nose taking in their scent as deep as I could and my heart just melted. For just a split second, they were there by me as I let their memories fill my mind. I only allowed myself to mourn sparsely which many said isn't healthy but the rest of the time I kept my mind and self occupied. In the first few years after their deaths, the grief almost destroyed me but my people brought me back from the brink of self destruction.

"Mama? Why do you cry?" Hazel's innocent voice says behind me.

"Because my heart is broken, Mija," I whispered in pain.

"But why, Mama? You're not supposed to be sad. When you're sad then everyone is sad," Octavio said.

"I know, babies. Mommy tries but some days are harder than others. I just miss you so much, mi amores." I can feel the words getting choked up in my mouth.

"We love you, Mama," Hazel tells me or maybe it was my mind playing more tricks on me. I couldn't tell anymore nor did I care.

"I love you both so much." I promise, closing my eyes, willing my mind to feel their touch, just the light pressure of their hands on my shoulders but nothing is all I feel.

"Please don't go," I beg their ghosts but neither respond and I am once again left alone with nothing but my own sorrow and pain.

After a few more hours of sitting and mourning my children, I wiped my face and stood up brushing my tunic off. I needed to check on the children of Mictlan and make sure that they are okay.

******

Turning away from the glass table, I took a moment and a deep breath to calm myself as this day was always painful to endure. Hiding it from all the watchful eyes was a necessity as ruler of the realm, I would have more time for my continual mourning when this spiritual holiday over over.

I quickly turn back when the hair on the back of my neck raise in alert. My eyes scanned the table. I watch my souls move about in the human realm merrily. The table was a unique tool for ruling, even being able to pinpoint souls if I felt the need necessary. My magic had the ability to turn the world into a 3D image as if I was right there amongst them, similar to watching a movie but more realistic. I was not omnipresent like the Creator of the Universe.

If I felt that there was something wrong with a soul or if one lagged behind, I could come here and look on at them. Were the need to arise from checking in on them to retrieve them then this layout would pinpoint whoever I was searching for across the world but my tether to them would bring us together.

I pulled Layla and Paca up checking in on them to see that they were having the time of their lives with her parents. She greedily, like the child she is, stuffed her face full of buttered tortillas as Paca smacked her lips, annoyed. Layla teased her, pouncing on top of her, effectively stealing her food while she pouted and her parents laughed.

Chuckling, I turned away to go back out into Mictlan where the adults were preparing for the return of the children in exchange for their departure for the next twenty-four hours.

A sharp pain like a shockwave went throughout my body, causing me to cry out and double over. Some of the souls came to my assistance.

"Your Majesty, are you all right?" Juan asked, and I looked up to see a bunch of faces staring at me worried.

Taking in their concerns, I smiled and straightened up, "Yeah..." I brushed them and the pain off, forcing myself to stand up. "I think I misstepped. Truly, I'm all right," I lied.

Something felt off but I couldn't show it, I tried to mull it over in my mind but I couldn't shake that something was wrong. I reached out through my tether to the souls and felt nothing out of the ordinary. In fact, I felt nothing at all... *That's odd.* I thought to myself, shaking it off waiting for the kids to return through the gates of Mictlan.

I stood at the gate with expectant family members waiting for the children to come back through the gate. Crickets would be better to hear than the hushed whispers of the worried adults that stood behind me.

Dong! Dong! Dong! The Clock chimed behind me and my brow furrowed with mixed emotions. The children always came home on time. Their spirit animals ensured it, they knew the dangers of not returning as well.

"Your Majesty, where are the children?" A soul calmly but worriedly asked.

"I'm sure they will be along at any moment. You know how excited they can get when they are allowed to return to the land of the living," I answered.

Taking a deep breath I closed my eyes, reaching out through the tether to feel the connection with the children.

Nothing...

The worry didn't set in until Paca came limping across the marigold bridge injured. "Paca?" I muttered confused. "Where's Layla?"

Paca whimpered and collapsed at my feet.

"Mic, where are the children?"

The smell of burnt flesh filled my nostrils as I knelt down to examine the spirit animal. The only thing capable of injuring one is a Soul Eater and their stench reeked on Paca. I laid my hands on her, focusing my energy visualizing her skin mending under my fingers until I felt she was once again whole. The souls watched with bated breath waiting for answers about their children.

My mind reached into Paca's as she sat there, watching and searching her thoughts. How did I not know the children and spirit animals were attacked? I am tethered to all things in Mictlan but to not even get a single goosebump? It just didn't make any sense to me.

Layla came into my vision, she was chasing Paca and playing along the way back to Mictlan. A sweet lullaby hummed through the night distracting Layla but Paca's hackles raised in alarm. The full moon began to fade and darkness started to shroud around them.

"Paca? What's wrong? What is it?" Layla whimpered in fear.

Her jaguar was more focused on what was hunting them than what Layla was saying. Her ferocious roars sounded in warning at whatever was coming in their direction.

Then a loud banshee wail surrounded them, and the weeping laughter of La Llorona filled the remaining silence. Her deathly glow was unmistakable as she came into view, humming Layla into a trance. Paca swiped her paw at her but she easily dodged her attacks.

"Foolish protector! You cannot save her! None of your spirit animal kinsmen can! The children are mine!"

Her malicious laugh sent a wave of nausea through me as I turned around to eyes full of questions.

"The children, Your Majesty…are they okay?" one soul asked.

Steadying my breathing, I looked at the eager crowd, "No…no, they are not okay. My people, my family…" My voice trailed off for a moment, "The children have been kidnapped by La Llorona."

Gasps and cries rang throughout the crowd, the voices rose in volume with questions upon questions. The panic was already setting in, threatening to take over my people by storm.

I raised my hands, "Everyone...please let me explain." But my words fell on deaf ears, with a voice of authority and using my ability, I raised my voice and thundered like a goddess, "SILENCE!"

Everyone fell silent, some even bowing before me for fear they angered me.

"I will bring the children back."

"What should we do, Your Majesty?" a young man's soul asked.

"You are to go about business as usual. This mission is too dangerous because she has the Soul Eaters backing her and I could not bear the thought of losing a single one of you," I explained.

Franco, a burly man with a thick mustache came forward through the crowd, "We would die for our children, even a forever death, if it meant that they would come home safe."

He knelt in allegiance to me and I took his hand, pulling him to his feet, "My friend, I have friends that have powerful friends on the other side as well. Please let me get to the bottom of this. I swear to you all on the graves of my children...I will bring each and every child home before midnight of All Souls Day. Now I know it will be hard but you all must be going before you miss out on your only day of the year to reunite with your loved ones. If you do not show up, they will not understand."

They nodded and hesitantly began to walk through the gates of Mictlan, some putting on brave faces while others wore theirs with no shame.

Blessings fell upon me as each and every soul passed by on their way to the human realm. Blessed with prayers of safety and victory, I watched them and their spirit animals cross the marigold bridge into the land of the living. I had twenty-fours hours to find, rescue, and bring home millions of souls.

Yeah, no pressure...no pressure at all. I thought to myself.

All Souls Day

I don't take things for granted, because everything feels more fragile. It's made me wonder about mortality and how long you've got somebody in the world. I'm more fearful than I used to be.
- Robin Gibb

I rode on the back of my pegasus, Paella, following Paca across the marigold bridge, curious to see where we would end up. Imagine my surprise when we came out in New Orleans and made our way down the French Quarter. Goosebumps arose across the back of my neck and arms at the thought of running into someone I had not seen in a very long time.

"Oooo cher...Hell must have frozen over if the Queen of Souls is here gracing our presence in New Orleans," Papa Legba chuckled, leaning back against an old brick and mortar building in the alleyway we were passing.

He was hidden by the darkness but I held my head high and remained silent, waiting for him to come forward. And out he came in all his swagger, always the fashionable Voodoo King in his zoot suit. I have always loved him in pinstripes. Salt and pepper cornrows draping from under his top hat, little voodoo dolls hung all over his suit jacket. Papa Legba strolled up to my leg, stroking the neck of my pegasus as he looked up at me. His face almost matched mine except his skull face only went down to exaggerate the extended top teeth below the nose.

The Voodoo King took my tattooed black hand into his midnight callused ones. The contrast was like night and day between us. He lifted my hand to his lips and his lips brushed against my knuckles in a soft kiss.

"It has been so long since I have felt the touch of your skin under my hands in what feels like a millenia, my lady." I let his fingers trace the patterns on the inside of my hand.

"My love. It has been a long time since I have seen you. New Orleans is not the safest when the veil between the living and the dead is so thin." Paella stomped her hoove on the ground, snorting and shaking her head. Papa Legba chuckled at the pegasus' tantrum. "Paella, you look as gorgeous as the day I brought you to Mic, always such a good girl," he said.

It was hard to look at him. When I stared at his face, all I could see were our twins. They looked much more like him than me. I swore I would never return to this wretched place once it took my babies from me, yet here I am.

Flashes of that awful day overcame my mind and thoughts.

The gates of Mictlan opened up as the children filed out to go back to be with their families for one day. Hazel and Octavio each took one of my hands as we ventured out to New Orleans to see their father. Their giggles and smiles filled my vision, warming my heart.

When we came out on the other side, chaos surrounded us as Soul Eaters and supernatural creatures were at war. Quickly, I rushed the children to their father's home.

The Voodoo King met us outside in front, "What are you doing here, cher? There's a revolt happening. The Soul Eaters are trying to overthrow us. It's too dangerous for you all to be here."

"But Papa, it's the only night we can be with you as a family," Hazel cried, big tears falling from her eyes.

"Cher, there are some really bad creatures that will hurt you and your brother, they are the only thing that can hurt any of us. It's just not safe."

"If they're after everyone then the souls of my people are in danger too. I need to make sure everyone is okay."

"That's what their spirit animals are for, they will get the children's souls back to Mictlan safely. You and the children need to flee here immediately. It's not safe anywhere in this realm. Reports have been coming in from all over the world about the Soul Eaters attacking in full force," Papa Legba warned.

"Fine. Children, we are going to get you back home where you'll be safe."

Octavio yanked his hand from mine screaming, "No! I want to stay with Papa! I want to be a family!"

We were interrupted by the hissing of the Soul Eaters coming down the alleyway blocking our escape. The Voodoo King and I pushed the kids behind us as we drew our scythe knives from our hips and I hissed back in warning at the creatures.

"Don't come out of this house for any reason," Legba warned the kids, shoving them inside. "They should be safe inside my home. Are you ready, cher?"

"Are you, old man?" I teased as we charged the Soul Eaters at full force. Our knives shredded them into oblivion, literally as they turned into piles of dust.

It felt like hours had passed since the battle ensued when the screams of Hazel filled our ear and we rushed into Papa Legba's home, the Soul Eater laughed as it consumed the last of Hazel's body and soul.

I shrieked, watching my child being absorbed into the body of the vile creature that stood before me. "MY BABIES!!!" I wailed.

Charging it, slicing and shredding, trying to pull my children from it but as it evaporated into dust, the reality set in that my children were dead and gone along with the Soul Eater.

My body fell limp onto the floor of the home, the knives clinking onto the ground alongside me.

I babbled nonsensically, "They were supposed to be safe here...my babies...they're gone.

Papa Legba knelt down, shaking me, but I was empty, my soul vanished along with my children that night. I forced every soul to return to Mictlan immediately and didn't open the gates for the next few years until I knew it was safe. But I have never been the same since then. The last moments with my children still haunt me until this day."

"Mic? Cher, are you okay?" He shook my hand, pulling me from my memory.

"Papa Legba something terrible has happened. I am following the lead of what seems to be the only surviving spirit animal that's left."

"What do you mean, Mi Calaca?" The Voodoo King stood back, confused by my words.

"The souls of children from Mictlan are missing. The only lead I have is from Paca here. She faced off with La Llorona and her pet Soul Eaters and barely escaped death to warn me of what happened. If I don't have them back across the marigold bridge by midnight tonight..." The lump caught in my throat and there was a hitch in my breath.

Papa Legba looked at me sympathetically as I slumped over in defeat, "Cher." His hand reached up and his thumb ran across my tattooed face, "I will help you find your children. Together we will save them, cher."

I grasped his hand in mine, "No matter the cost. Swear to me that you will do whatever to bring them home, Papa Legba. I can't lose the souls of every child of Mictlan. It'll be the end of me, I cannot bear the loss of even one more child." Tears fell down my face, "I can't feel them or their spirit animals anywhere. There's nothing but a giant void where my heart used to be."

"You have my word, cher. I will do whatever we have to do. Even if I have to crawl through the pits of Hell itself to bring them home, I will."

"Thank you, my love," I uttered my gratitude.

Papa Legba backed away from me, "I must leave you for now but I will return to you. Do not leave Paella's and Paca's sides, they will protect you while I go retrieve information about what La Llorona is up to tonight."

My hands ran down Paella's mane absentmindedly. "That was quite odd and even abrupt, don't you say, Paella?" She stomped indignant, "Yeah well, you were always biased toward him anyway," I huffed back.

~ Papa Legba ~

Like the coward I was, I retreated to the shadows away from Mic. She was still as hauntingly beautiful as the day I met her. Completely tattooed from head to toe with the skeletal features only the Queen of Souls could have. Her dark eyes shone under the moonlight and her long black hair hung down her back with a braided crown around her forehead. My Spanish Viking that made my heart ache at the sight of her every time.

Talking to her, touching her hand felt like new life had been breathed back into me. Has it really been decades since we last saw one another? The loss of the twins nearly drove her mad and I was unable to be with her in all that time. While I could communicate with the other side, I was not of Aztec origin which forbade me from entering the gates of Mictlan.

Turning against the brick wall, I leaned my forehead against the cold wall, wanting to bash my head against it. I was too late to warn her and all the children had been kidnapped. Now how was I supposed to help her? She already blames me for the death of the twins. If she finds out that I knew about the attacks on the souls, she'll end up blaming me for that too.

I let out a breath I hadn't realized I had been holding in when a voice whispered over my shoulder, "Coward."

"Shut up!" I told my tormentor.

"She'll never forgive you. You'll always be the reason your children are dead. It's all your fault," it kept on.

"I said shut up!" I hollered at it as a couple walked by.

They paused, staring weirdly at me. "Mister, are you okay?" the guy asked.

"Yeah." I pointed at my ear, "Sorry, arguing with someone," I lied, trying to play it off.

"Oh...okay," he answered as his girlfriend squeezed a little tighter onto his arm.

Tonight always takes its toll on me but seeing Mic after all this time and on the anniversary of our kids' deaths was making it harder. I'll give myself time to pull it together then I need to find

Mic and help her get the souls of the children of Mictlan back.

~ Mic ~

Mixed emotions rolled through me at coming face to face with the Voodoo King again after all this time apart from one another. Anger, pity, and even sorrow swirled inside. I wasn't sure how I would feel but mostly loneliness gnawed at me. I'd give anything to let him hold me the rest of the night as we remember our babies together. The only option I had left was to go where all monsters in New Orleans go during Dia de los Muertos. Marie Laveau's bar, The Voodoo Lair was the place all other worldly beings and creatures ended up at some point when visiting here.

I need a fireball or a tequila shot anyway to steady my nerves after everything that has happened.

The guard took one look at me and bowed, "Your Majesty...welcome."

"Thanks, Oliver. Can you inform Marie that I am here?" I asked and he replied with a nod.

The club was full of all kinds of creatures, Sandmen, witches, vampires and shifters watched me with a look of curiosity as I made my way to the bar to get a drink.

I stalked up to the bar and laid my pesos down, "I'll take a shot of fireball and a few of tequila. The good stuff too, Nalley, not that cheap stuff."

"Mic, I haven't seen you step foot out of Mictlan since the death of your twins." My eyes blackened and I hissed back at her ignorance. "Forgive me, Your Majesty, I meant no disrespect to you, just that everyone is surprised to see you after all this time."

The thick cajun accent of Marie Laveau spoke up behind me, "Forgive her, Mic. She lets her mouth get the best of her still, these younger generation creatures. They're like children, they don't think before they speak." She spoke the words laced with warning while staring at Nalley.

Nalley quickly moved on down the bar to serve another customer as Marie reached over the bar, grabbing a bottle of tequila and a couple shot glasses. Waltzing off to a table in the corner of the bar, I followed behind her.

"Marie..." I started but was cut off.

"I know why you're here, cher," she answered.

"You do?" I eyed her suspiciously.

"Oh yes, someone or something has stolen souls of the children of Mictlan and a spirit animal led you straight to New Orleans?" she answered.

"How did you know what happened to the children?"

"Because I am the one who saved Paca so she could make it back to Mictlan to warn you." Marie held a shot glass out to me, as I took it and we both clinked the glasses before downing our shots.

"Then you know La Llorona took them but do you know why?" I asked.

"Rumor has it she seeks her children, the very children she murdered and that you care for in Mictlan. These monsters have all been buzzing about the chaos she has caused in all circles, not just yours. Every year, a different species of kids have been going missing during these three sacred days when the veil is at its thinnest." She took another shot before continuing, "She's not mentally stable. It never ends well by the time we find the children. I'm not even sure she knows what she's doing until it's too late, then she's sucked back into purgatory until the next year when she can leave again. You find her kids and you just might be able to save the souls of the children you maintain."

"How could she possibly capture the souls of all those children? One woman's spirit is not that powerful."

"She is when she is using the Soul Eaters. The rumor says that she struck a deal with their leader and they're helping her."

My mouth dropped in shock, "She wouldn't sacrifice other souls of children just to get her hands on her children's souls?"

"What would you sacrifice for the chance to have your children back, cher?" Marie countered.

"Touché, I guess," I answered, downing another shot of tequila.

She stood up, leaving the bottle of tequila on the table for me. "This one is on the house tonight. If I can be of assistance, let me know."

The hair on the back of my neck stood up, I knew who it was before I even looked, "You found me fast, Papa Legba. Your friends on the other side sure are chatty if you already have information for me."

"Cher, you're still as stubborn as the day I met you."

I held up a shot glass in agreement, "Well, mi amor, I would have brought Paca and Paella in but Marie frowns upon me bringing them inside."

"Won't you dance with me once more, cher?" the Voodoo King asked me with an extended hand.

My eyes looked at his hand hesitantly for a moment unsure. "One dance," I warned him.

He chuckled darkly. "Are you afraid of what you might feel after one dance?" he challenged.

My eyes rolled in response as the drums began to pick up the beat and our hips started to sway. The singer's voice was haunting as we kept with the pace of the music. Letting my eyes close, I let the beat just carry me away. Far, far away to a distant memory; possibly one of my most cherished ones that I held on to now.

Fog covered the streets of New Orleans and the spirits roamed amongst the living. I wander through the streets alongside them, watching the reunion of the living and the dead once again.

The beautiful voice of Georgia Jean was drifting all around us with music that made your hips sway to the beat of the drum. My feet lead me to the Voodoo Lair of Marie Laveau.

I went to open the door to let myself inside when a security guard grabbed my arm to stop me.

"Excuse me, ma'am, but you can't go in there," he said but my blackened eyes were the only warning he needed to let go of me.

"My apologies, madam, I did not realize..." his voice trailed off as I walked past him and through the doors.

Georgia Jean was singing another number as I situated myself on the barstool and watched in awe, letting her voice enthrall me.

"My, my...looks like I have been graced with the presence of the most beautiful goddess being present tonight," the Voodoo King of New Orleans said softly.

"Papa Legba, your reputation precedes you, I see," I said dryly.

Over the years, I had heard many things about the Voodoo King, the man who could speak to his 'friends' on the other side. A charmer and gifted silver-tongued man with a deep voice that felt like velvet to your ears.

He chuckled at my words, "Aw, cher, I hope they are good things you have heard."

The bartender slid me a shot of tequila, and I took a sip. "Depends on who you ask, I guess," I answered bluntly.

He grabbed his chest as if he had been shot, "I'm hurt. Does that mean that I don't stand a chance with the Queen of Souls?"

It was my turn to laugh this time, "That completely depends."

"How so?" he asked, intrigued as I flagged down the bartender for another drink.

"If you can prove those rumors wrong," I answered bluntly.

He slid closer to me, pulling up a seat on the barstool, "Well, I look forward to that challenge, cher."

The Voodoo King's voice, whispering in my ear, shook me from the memory, "You still look stunning, cher. I've missed you. In all these years, there has never been another, only you," he promised.

"Lying doesn't suit you, mi amor. Let's just dance and not talk. You'll ruin it."

"Tsk, tsk, tsk... Always so skeptical the Queen of Souls still is after all these years. Your heart has hardened," he accused, his hand tightening around my waist holding me against him. "There has never been another for me, only you, Mic. We are bound to one another for all eternity, even if you have left me to mourn alone since the children's..."

I pushed away from him, "Stop it. Don't you dare say it!" I hollered full of fire and vengeance, slapping him across the face.

The bar stilled and my cheeks flamed hot and my chest heaved up and down angrily. We stared at one another without saying a word. I grabbed the tequila and poured me another shot, downing it before tossing it behind me.

"Well, this was fun but I think I'm better on my own, Papa Legba. I think it would be better for you to just leave me be from here on out," I warned before storming off out of the bar.

Throwing the bar door open, the cold air engulfed me, jarring me from my brief haze as my head cleared. I was harsh with Legba and I paused outside the door thinking about going back inside but shook my head instead and made my way to Paella and Paca who waited for me.

Marie Laveau waltzed out of the bar and stared me up and down.

"Oh spare me your lecture, Marie."

Shaking her head, "No lecture needed. I think you're doing a good job at beating yourself up still, even after all these years…you blame not just yourself but Papa Legba for what happened that night."

"Don't push me, old friend. I'm not in the mood for it."

"Friend to friend, cher?" We eyed one another as she continued, "He has been beating himself up ever since it happened. Many nights, I've picked him up out of the gutter drunk as a skunk and rambling like a mad fool. You're not the only one suffering the loss of my niece and nephew."

"He should have warned me! I wouldn't have left Mictlan if I had known…"

She cut me off, "What? Known that we were all under attack that night? News flash, Mic, we were all a little busy and unable to do much of anything other than protect one another's back," Marie screamed frustrated. "Sometimes you can be so blind and selfish!"

I jumped, taken aback by her insinuation, "Well, I won't bother you again, Marie."

"Wait. I didn't mean that, Mic. Look, Rumor has it that the Soul Eaters and La Llorona are hiding out deep in the bayou."

"Okay, thanks," I mumbled, climbing up onto Paella's back.

"Mic, you cannot go at this alone. They will kill you! Goddess or not, they can kill you! Cher, you need back up! Come back inside and we'll recruit some help and go at this together."

She reached out and grabbed my hand, squeezing it tightly. She cared, always has, and being the sister of the Voodoo King was a challenge in itself. Marie knew her brother better than I did.

Tears welled up in my eyes, threatening to spill over. "I'm sorry, Marie. This is something I have to do on my own. I appreciate your help though, old friend.

She nodded in understanding, "Well since I can't convince you otherwise, take these. You'll need them."

Reaching into her back pockets, Marie pulled my old scythe knives out. The ones I had given to Papa Legba a long time ago during our courtship.

"Thank you," I said gratefully, spinning them around in my hand.

The movement was familiar and comfortable, like I never stopped using them. My hands tightened on Paella's reins as my tongue clicked and my heels dug in, signaling for her to get a move on. I gave a quick glance behind me and Marie watched me leave, sadness and pity was the last look on her face that I would see tonight.

~ Papa Legba ~

Some of the streets of the French Quarter had become barren which was a mixture of odd and rare. Down at the end of the block, a woman with long black hair and a tattered white dress stood facing me. I couldn't make out her face in this dark lighting and at this distance.

I made my way over to her, figuring she was a lost soul wandering about.

"Cher? Are you lost?" I cautiously called.

Her quiet wail started to get louder and I froze where I stood at the realization of who this soul was.

"Llorona, I heard you have been busy tonight."

Her menacing laugh sent a chill in my heart, "Papa Legba, I've been looking for you."

"Awe, cher. I'm touched but I do not believe we have any business with one another," I smiled, keeping her at a distance.

When she would step forward, I would step back and when she stepped to the side, I would side step each one.

"Are you afraid of me, Voodoo King?" she asked, amused.

"No, Cher, just keeping my safety a priority. I do not trust you. I will not join you but you need to return the children to Mictlan before things get ugly," I warned her.

"You know I cannot do that until I find my children," she answered.

"Llorona, you have caused so much pain over the years at the expense of other children. I know your pain, I understand it."

She stalked as we paced back and forth in a circular pattern, "The enemy of my enemy is my friend, I guess. I heard about you and the Queen of Souls, Papa Legba- how the Soul Eaters devoured your children."

The reminder of the death of my children only fueled my rage that I kept behind a locked door inside of me. There was something about Llorona though, she wasn't completely too far gone, only lost.

"You heard the boasting of those monsters but you do not accept what they are, they disgust you. I can see it in the way you speak about them. Let me tell you a little about the Queen of Souls and our children. At first, the children were with their mother full time but then as they started to get older we thought that one of the twins living in the human realm while the other was with their mother would work. We even switched off but their twin bond was too strong, they struggled being without one another.

That night that they died, we were meeting to come to a better solution to be a family but then they were taken away. You pairing up with the

Soul Eaters makes you no better than they are. They will lead to your ultimate demise, Llorona."

"Are you trying to empathize with me, Papa Legba?" she coaxed.

"I am trying to stop you from making another mistake, cher. Because Mic will not stop until she brings every soul back to Mictlan."

"Then I will make sure to destroy her if she gets in my way. You should have chosen my side, Papa Legba. Maybe I would have spared her...or not? But now you'll never know," she laughed evilly before disappearing.

I looked around for her but she was gone. This was much bigger than we thought. We needed help, the only kind that New Orleans can offer at that.

~ Mic ~

The bayou was a tricky place to end up. Unfortunately for me, the souls of the children of Mictlan counted on me. Paca stalked warily beside Paella as I rode on her back. Her hackles raised, showing she was alert to our surroundings. I couldn't shake the feeling that already we were not alone, being watched if not hunted ourselves.

"Paca..." The jaguar looked at me. "Track the children," I commanded as Layla's spirit animal took off sprinting and my heels dug into the side of Paella encouraging her onward, galloping behind Paca. Without the connection, I had to rely on Paca to find her child's soul since they were deeply connected.

Sulfur putrefied the air around us, which meant that we were closing in on their lair. The moon was full but was not its usual silver glow. Instead, it was one of blood red, a harvest moon.

Darkness seems to start creeping in from all around as Paella reared up, neighing in defiance at the shadows. Soul Eaters snarled and swiping their claws hungrily at us. Paca roared, swiping her claws back at them. Spirit animals were enchanted with the ability to protect their charges, so Paca's claws were made from the same material as my scythe blades.

I dismounted Paella. If there was going to be a fight, then she needed me off her back to defend herself and me as well, if needed.

Pulling the scythe knives from their sheathes on my hips, I flipped them upside down with my fists squared up, ready to fight. Letting my wrathful side take over, my eyes blackened, switching over to that beautiful night vision. I could make out each and every Soul Eater's position.

"All right, you ugly pieces of trash, let's dance," I egged on.

The first one came straight at me as I side-stepped and pivoted around it, letting my knife in my right hand sink in the middle of its back. It shrieked and I let my sharp blade glide down its spine as I came fully around and sunk my other knife into its neck, twisting the metal deep within until it started disintegrating.

"Awe, Cher, I see your fighting skills haven't wavered in all these years," the Voodoo King laughed from the shadows.

He pulled his sword from its holder that the cane provided, charging a Soul Eater, slicing its head clean off instantly. At that, the dance began in full force. The Voodoo King and the Queen of Souls reunited once again in a battle for the souls we care for, against the evil forces that walk this fallen earth.

Souls from the other side that lived in New Orleans came out of the shadows of the bayou, chanting and fighting alongside Papa Legba and I. Witches and other supernatural creatures that had died at the hands of the Soul Eaters were back for revenge and there was no escape from them. Some tried to flee but the dead witches blocked them in, drawing their power from the land, using ancient magic that had been lost after their extinction.

Back to back, we fought beside one another to defeat the Soul Eaters, just like old times.

"You need to go and find the children, Mic. We can handle this, you have the spirits of New Orleans behind you," the Voodoo King urged.

I looked at him bewildered, "I will not leave you here to fight these creatures."

He huffed exasperated, "Look, we're to help you get to La Llorona. We're simply here to clear the path. Now go!" he ordered.

"Fine," I answered and started to turn to leave but paused, turning back.

I grabbed his face, smashing my lips against his desperate for one more kiss from him.

He smiled, "What was that for?"

I shrugged, "Just in case."

We shared a brief smile, locking eyes. I whistled for Paella. As she ran by, I grabbed a fistful of her mane and yanked myself onto her back as she galloped off out of the battle between the souls of New Orleans and the Soul Eaters.

It wasn't long before I was within earshot of the banshee screams and wailing filling the quiet bayou as we watched as the trees and the Spanish moss provided the perfect shelter.

Llorona was pacing back and forth as child after child's soul was brought forward but to her dismay they were not her children. Off in the distance, two children were shaking and holding onto one another, whispering back and forth. The more I examined them, the more I could see the family resemblance. La Llorona's face was distorted with her demon side but the similarities were there.

"MIGUEL! SOPHIA!" She cried out but the children just sat on the ground huddled together, whimpering. "If none of you are my babies or know where they are, then I will be left with no choice but to hand you all over to the Soul Eaters," she threatened.

The Soul Eaters hissed, reaching out to grab at the children hungrily causing them to recoil in fear, screaming out louder.

Disgusted, I marched through the thicket and out into the clearing, "Llorona! That's enough!" I ordered.

She spun around in anger at me, "Who are you to challenge me?"

My wrath began to take over and my eyes blackened as my Aztec warrior side came to fruition, ready for battle once more.

"I am Mictecacihuatl. Queen of Souls, protector of Mictlan and you have stolen what is mine. The souls of the children of Mictlan belong to me in their land of afterlife. What right do you have to take them on their sacred night of reunions with their descendants?" I challenged back.

"You." She pointed at me with her deadened finger, "You are the one who has kept my babies from being reunited with me," she accused then threatened. "I should punish you for the pain I have suffered all these centuries for your selfishness."

I shook my head, "You are mistaken, Llorona. The children can choose to leave Mictlan or not but your children do not always have interest in returning to this realm because they have no descendants to visit. If they do come to the earthly realm they simply roam about exploring. Their family line died when you murdered them."

"Lies!!" she wailed in her high pitched banshee scream. The children covered their ears in protection.

"It is true but your children are here, I will let you see them if you promise to let the others and their spirit animals go," I attempted to negotiate.

"You will return my children to me or I will annihilate every soul here along with their spirit animal. My Soul Eaters are very hungry and I'm not sure I can keep their hunger at bay any longer,"she warned back.

"You would kill every child in a second death, just to get back at me?" I said in disbelief.

"Yes!" she spat back, her words laced with venom.

She lunged forward, swiping her claws at my face. I jumped back out of her reach, spinning around and letting my blade glide across her petrified skin, ash and blackened blood spewing from the open cut.

Her screeches of pain were deafening to all around. Again and again, she struck at me with her elongated claws, taking out all of her anger and pain on me. I let her because I had anger and pain built up within me as well. We exchanged blow for blow until I grew tired of the song and dance with her.

Flipping into the air, I teleported behind her in surprise, wrapping my arm around her and my blade from my other hand under her throat.

"Even if it meant you would be murdering them all over again?"

She paused, taken back by the truth of my words. Her dark side seemed to fade as she stopped and really looked at the kids. The horror of self realization started to cross her mind.

Miguel and Sophia stood up and stepped forward, "Mama?" they both said, confused.

"Miguel? Sophia?" she exclaimed as tears slowly streamed down her cheeks.

"Mama! Mama!" They rushed her, wrapping their arms around her waist bravely.

"We missed you so much, Mommy!" Sophia cried.

Miguel didn't speak but held onto Llorona and his sister.

Llorona looked at the Soul Eaters, "The deal is off...release the spirit animals and the children!"

"No!" they hissed in unison.

Llorona pushed her children behind her as I flanked her, challenging the Soul Eaters alongside her.

"I said be gone from this place, vile creatures!" I ordered.

As they closed in, I held my knives up ready to fight when the sounds of witches chanting surrounded the bayou.

"You are trespassing on sacred ground," Papa Legba's voice rang.

"We do not take kindly to creatures coming after our children," Marie warned, her eyes whitened and shaking her rattle that she uses in her rituals.

The Soul Eaters recoiled, shrieking and hissing at them as they began to fade away. The souls of the ancestral covens that have passed over into the afterlife continued to follow them, leaving me with La Llorona and the children of Mictlan. Papa Legba came back into sight with the children's spirit animals. The children hugged their animals in relief. Some shed a few tears, still clearly scared of the events that had transpired.

Llorona looked up from her children apologetically at the other children and me, "No words can ever prove to you exactly how sorry I am for the pain I have caused each and every one of you. My only hope is that you will someday find it in your hearts to forgive me."

The children all looked at one another then back at her and nodded before following their spirit animals back home. The gate would be closing soon for another year, any soul left out in the realm would go mad, eventually wasting away into nothing.

"Mictecacihuatl, Queen of Souls, can they stay with me?" Llorona pleaded.

"This realm cannot sustain their souls. They cannot survive in this realm, that is why it is so imperative for them and others to get back before midnight when the gates of Mictlan are closed for another year," I explained.

She wept into her children, resting her head on their heads. "I am not sure I can do what you are requesting of me. I have only just found them after all this time," she confessed.

"I can give you some time to catch up with them but before midnight comes, they will return with me. That much is final. You do not want to fight with me on this, Llorona," I warned her.

"What she is offering is a gift, cher," Marie interrupted. "After everything that has happened, that could have happened, I suggest that you take the gift given to you."

Llorona nodded in response, ushering her children off to the side, sitting on the bayou floor. They chatted animatedly amongst one another as I watched on in supervision, unsure of how much I could really trust her.

"You are foolish, cher," Marie started but I held up a hand, stopping her. "For my children of Mictlan, I would give my life over and over again and again for them. There is nothing I wouldn't have done for them, Marie." I turned to face her, "I do not regret my choices I have made but... I appreciate you and Legba coming to my rescue with the souls of the witches of New Orleans. Most likely, I wouldn't have survived if you all hadn't shown up like you did," I confessed to her.

We leaned forward, our foreheads laying against one another, our show of affection and love. She will always be like a sister to me, no matter what or how many years pass by.

"I think we can take the win tonight. The witches will hunt the Soul Eaters until they're either dead or far, far away from New Orleans. They will not set foot on our land again."

We turned back and watched Llorona and her children's reunion some more. We admired how forgiving and loving children can be to a parent, no matter how much one can fail their own blood.

"Nor will they hurt any soul of Mictlan. We will be better and more diligent about the future, both in Mictlan and in the realm of the living," I vowed.

From the ashes of the Soul Eaters rose orbs of light, we watched in awe as souls began to expand from those orbs. Souls of people that the

Soul Eaters had absorbed were free. It was as if a curse had been lifted, a curse that no one knew about from what I could recollect.

Maybe when Llorona murdered her kids and then committed suicide in all her grief, it caused some kind of chain effect.

"Llorona..."

"Yes?" she replied.

"Did you say anything when you died? Cursing your husband and his mistress?" I asked.

She looked away ashamed, "I did but I would rather not speak those words again for fear I would enact something worse."

I nodded, "Fair enough."

It was a beautiful sight. My heart leaped, searching the crowd for the twins with budding hope.

Then my heart sank when I realized that they were not among the crowd of freed souls.

Bravely, I put on a strong front to Marie, "Well, looks like the job is not done yet. These souls need to be ferried but I can only take my people. Can you see to the rest?"

"Of course, Mic. You take care of yourself, okay?"

"You too, Marie. See you next year," I promised.

"I'm holding you to that," she laughed, walking into the crowd.

"Paella, take the souls of Mictlan home. I'll be there shortly." My pegasus started ushering the souls to follow her without another word.

Epilogue: Destiny

The seat of Realization is within and the seeker cannot find it as an object outside him. That seat is bliss and is the core of all beings. Hence it is called the Heart.
- Ramana Maharshi

Llorona held onto her children weeping, not wanting to let them go. I looked at her with pity.

"Miguel, Sophia, listen to me." She knelt down in front of her children, her hands rubbing up and down their arms absentmindedly. "Mic is going to take you home with the other children now. I am so sorry for what I did to you. I am sorry for the pain I caused everyone. Mama is not an evil person, just misguided, my loves."

The children looked at one another as Miguel said, "Mama, Mic helped us forgive you a long time ago. We're not upset with you anymore. We've been waiting for you to forgive yourself so you can be free to join us in Mictlan finally."

Sophia took Llorona's face in her hands, "Abuelita and Abuelito have taken such good care of us in Mictlan, you would love it there. It's always peaceful and everyone is happy. We feast every day with one another. There is no sorrow or pain, only peace and comfort."

"I wish I could join you both but I cannot cross the threshold of the marigold bridge without paying for my crimes. There are rules to this afterlife, my loves," Llorona wept.

I stepped forward to intercede, "As Queen of Souls, I cannot look past the crimes of kidnapping the souls of the children of Mictlan and the murders of the innocents over the centuries. You are correct, Llorona, for what you've done, you have to answer for your crimes. Here is my sentencing: La Llorona you are hereby exiled to earth with the task of saving children from Soul Eaters for seven years to atone for all the lives you have taken. But every year when the veil is at its thinnest, for twenty-four hours, you will be reunited with your children on All Saints Day during Dia de los Muertos. Once you have served your time, you will be able to cross the marigold bridge into Mictlan to spend all eternity with your children and family."

Llorona stood up and brushed her knees off, "Your Majesty, your offer is fair and most kind. I accept your sentencing."

Nodding in mutual agreement, I looked down at her children, "Miguel and Sophia, it's time to say goodbye to your mother. Paella will escort you home before the gates to Mictlan close for the next year."

Llorona and I helped them onto Paella's back as they said their goodbyes, "Bye, Mama." Sophia hugged her tightly.

"See you next year, Mama." Miguel smiled back at her through watery eyes as he wrapped his arms around his sister, taking the reins to the bridle.

"Paella, you must hurry and get them through the gates. No matter the cost. Go! Go now!" I swatted her on the rump as she neighed in annoyance, taking flight back to Mictlan.

I turned to face Llorona, her features changed since being reunited with her children. She looked more young and vibrant, although I'm sure her dark side lurked somewhere within. That would take time to fade but if she kept up with her sentencing by the end of the time served, she would no longer have it inside.

"I cannot thank you enough for all you've done to help me rectify the situation I put myself in, Mic," she said gratefully.

Taking a deep breath I nodded, "I wasn't so sure for a while there but honestly if you had not helped me defeat the Soul Eaters then I most likely would have failed."

"Actually I cannot take all the credit. Papa Legba was a part of the reason I saw past my ways. He told me about what happened with your twins. I can sympathize with your pain, seeing one of them from a distance only to have them ultimately ripped from your life forever. Although in your children's living life before they were killed by the Soul Eaters, one of them had to roam the earth with his father, the Voodoo Prince and the Princess of Mictlan. At least, you've been able to watch that child grow while being able to spend precious time with their sibling in Mictlan. It's not that bad of a trade off, you got to see them and be with them until the accident. You all got to be a family, even if it was only for a speck of time." Llorona confessed.

"Thank you," I said, shaking at her confession.

"Maybe you should forgive their father. It was neither of y'all's fault what happened with the Soul Eaters. Those things are just pure chaos and evil. He's still hurting just as much as you with the death of the twins," she admitted.

Tears welled in my eyes as I nodded unable to speak. Coughing to clear the giant lump in my throat, "I must be going. The gates are closing and the veil is regaining itself. Take care of yourself, Llorona. I'll be keeping a close eye on you."

I held my hand out to her as she stared at it. She smiled back at me, "I'll be seeing you soon, Mic."

After we parted ways, I wandered through the streets of New Orleans. Taking in the cool night's air. I knew where he was in the French Quarter, I knew he would be waiting like he did every year but I stopped meeting at our spot after the twins died. It was just too painful to face.

"The sunrises are always so beautiful after Dia de los Muertos is over," I whispered, stopping beside him.

"I think this is the most beautiful one I have ever seen now that you're here with me again," the Voodoo King answered.

"You know I can't stay. I have to get back to my people." I let out a longing breath, "I just wanted to say goodbye. You need to understand I don't blame you for what happened to our children. This world has fallen and evil creatures roam this realm. We always knew the risk of having them and letting them travel between the realms."

He nodded, "It was nice seeing you again. It has been too long, cher. I wish it had been under better circumstances. Seems like bad luck has always followed us. I'm not sure there is such a thing as a happy ending for the two of us, Mic."

I turned to leave, pausing shoulder to shoulder, facing the opposite direction from him. "I suppose not but don't you like playing the odds anyways..." I smiled as he glanced over at me.

"Ah, cher...there's no one else I would rather play the odds with than you," he confessed.

I took his hand and placed it over my beating heart, "You will always have my heart, mi amor."

He pulled my hand back to his lips, gently kissing them. "Until next year, cher?"

"Yes, indeed. It's a date." I winked playfully, walking away but still he held onto my hand tightly.

My breathing hitched at the thought of my leaving him after all this time. The separation didn't change how I truly felt about the Voodoo King of New Orleans. He pulled me back to him, face to face. I looked up at him as he smiled down at me.

"Would you grant me one kiss to help me endure the time until I see you again, cher?" Papa Legba whispered.

I smiled into his hand as he cupped my cheek, "Yes, something to keep the flame burning until the gates of Mictlan are open once again and I can be in your arms." His lips were soft as he held me for a few moments longer. "Until we meet again, mi amor."

~ Papa Legba ~

I sat outside of Cafe Du Monde drinking coffee, replaying the events that have passed. My mind was still processing everything but relieved that the souls of all the children would now be safe.

Extraordinary butterflies fluttered about in the morning light. A sign that all the souls of Mictlan had returned safely home. It was the only peace I was given every year after Dia de los Muertos.

"Such a beautiful morning, don't you agree?" A gentleman smiled, sitting across from me.

I looked around me, he wasn't there a second ago. Something about him wreathed him in power but a pure energy of good.

Tilting my head in confusion, "Yes, indeed. Do I know you, sir?"

"You know, I did this as a gift to Mictecacihuatl. She has always been a faithful angel." He continued, "She was one of my most loyal soldiers which is why I chose her for this position. I knew she would do whatever was needed, no matter the consequences."

"Mic is more than loyal and she has suffered extensively over her long reign as Queen of Souls," I added.

"Ah, yes. I know," he answered sadly.

Realization came over me at who this individual was and I didn't know at that moment if I should be humbled or scared.

"Yet, you did nothing, Creator," I accused. He raised an eyebrow at me, my mouth agape in shock at what I just said. "Forgive me, Creator, it has been a rough few days in the realms."

The Creator nodded, "Not nothing. She could have come to me but she chose not to. Painful as it may be, it was to serve a greater purpose and I have protected your children in this time. They have not suffered or been in pain."

"Are they happy? Do they know their mother and I miss them? That we love them and think about them every single moment we breathe?" I said breathlessly.

He smiled a knowing smile, "Very much so. They understood why things happened the way they did. In my realm, they know no pain or suffering."

His words pained me as much as they brought hope to my old dead heart. Looking into his eyes, I could see peace and feel it radiating from him.

"Why are you here, Creator?" I asked bluntly.

He chuckled, his wrinkles extending at his eyes, "I am here to offer you a chance to be a family once more."

"A gift as gracious as this, what's the catch?" I asked suspiciously. "There's always a catch."

"Not the kind of catch you're thinking of, Legba. You see, after you all freed those souls from the Soul Eaters, they will all be wandering the earth and that cannot happen. So I need someone to ferry the souls to their proper resting place. But I have to warn you, Papa Legba, you will still have to reside in the human realm until your time of death," the Creator offered.

"What about when I die? Where will my soul end up?" curiously, I asked.

"Depends on you and how the rest of your life goes. I can't tell you for sure because that would be technically cheating but if you continue on the path you've been on then I can't see why you can't spend eternity in Mictlan with your family.

"What do I have to do to accept?" I asked, my heart squeezed at the idea of being with my family again.

"Why just the same as when you make a deal with your friends on the other side. Just shake my hand, of course," he chuckled.

I reached across the table and took the Creator's hand without hesitation. In that moment, I felt a different kind of power surge through my veins and I couldn't help but wonder if this is what Mic felt when she underwent her transformation.

In the next moment, the Creator had vanished as if he was never there. But my eyes were open to a new sight, an angel stood by the table behind where the Creator sat just moments before.

"Papa Legba, if you would come with me," he said.

"Where are we going?" I asked.

"To your family," he answered.

~ Mic ~

After all the souls had been released and set free, I snapped my fingers transporting me back to the gates of Mictlan. As I crossed through them, the souls welcomed me back inside. Praise and thanks for saving all the children sounded all around. A giant feast awaited us all with my return. I blessed the food and said some words of healing and faith. Then the feast began and I watched my people enjoy one another, feeling the peace that Mictlan gives all souls that rest here.

My heart swelled with gratitude as I watched them all and knew, in that moment, it all had been worth it. My people were safe and we would move on from this and eventually this will be a distant memory.

"Mama..." a small voice said behind me and my body stilled.

It couldn't be...maybe I was finally losing it after everything that has happened but then I felt it- two small hands on my arms.

"Mama, won't you look at us?" another voice asked.

Tears fell down my cheeks. *Please don't be so cruel to me, my mind.* I cannot handle it. I realized everyone had fallen silent at the feast and gasps filled the silence as they all stared behind me.

Slowly, I turned around to see Hazel and Octavio standing there, an angel stood behind them.

"Mija? Mijo?" I wailed, snatching them up into my arms.

Everyone cheered in celebration, "But... how?" I asked, confused.

"The Creator appreciates everything you did to restore order to the human realm. As a gift from Him, he brought your children back to you," the angel answered.

Not a single hair on their heads was missing, nor did they carry even a scar from the events of that day.

"Your father will be so happy to see you both. I'm happy to have you back in my life, I have missed you two more than anything in the world."

"Starting the party without me, I see?" the Voodoo King laughed.

"Papa!" the kids yelled in unison rushing him.

"Wait a minute, how are you here when you're alive?" I questioned.

"The Creator doesn't like for families to have to be apart so he enabled Papa Legba to be able to travel to come back and forth between Mictlan and the human realm to fulfill his duties. This way you can be a family and cherish this second chance," the angel explained, smiling back.

We embraced one another, my family together once more. I looked over Legba's shoulder at the angel as he backed away and mouthed, *Thank you!*

He merely smiled and disappeared from sight. My people made room at the head of the table for my family to join, as we celebrated long into the day for the miracles and blessings that we were bestowed with this Dia de los Muertos.

About the Author

Kristen is a Native Texan, born and raised close to the heart of the great Lone Star State. Kristen is a full-time mother and housewife, as well as a Lupus Warrior. She has a passion for paranormal romance stories, which she finds herself writing in the most unexpected times and places.

Kristen enjoys exploring new types of characters such as Sandmen and Boogeymen, but prefers angels over any other fantasy being. She strongly believes her faith has granted her success that she never could've anticipated on her own, and it has encouraged her to focus her writing on the beings that God created.

Outside of writing, Kristen enjoys creating Art Journals that can be cross generational from thirteen to sixty years young.